WOUNDED
FOR MY
DESTINY

Wounded for my Destiny

Copyright 2018

William Belle jr and Tiffany Denmark Belle

ISBN 978-1-63227-280-5

SCR, Inc. Publishing

WOUNDED
FOR MY
DESTINY

Tiffany Denmark Belle
William Belle jr.

TABLE OF CONTENTS

INTRODUCTION

Survivor's guilt is a mental condition commonly linked to PTSD. It can occur after experiencing a traumatic event, such as war, a mass casualty assault, or even a fatal car accident. Feelings of *Why did I survive? What could I have done to save them? Maybe, if I wasn't there, they would they have lived?* Can be as painful as physical injuries. But, unlike physical injuries, survivor's guilt is an invisible wound to the psyche that can take months or even years to heal.

Survivor's guilt is as it sounds: it is an unshakable guilty feeling associated with surviving a traumatic event in which others died. Those with survivor's guilt, especially following a fatal car accident, often harbor feelings of resentment and shame for living; while others had to die. These feelings can affect everyday living, resulting in loss of appetite, inability to sleep, feelings of depression and anxiety, and loss of motivation.

Many individuals experience survivor's guilt, such as cancer survivors, those who lost a fellow service member, and those who were involved in an accident that took another's life. They ask questions like:

"Why am I still here?"
"Why did I survive?"
"Why them?"
"Why not me?"
"Why did this happen?"

This guilt is a common reaction to loss and other traumatic events, and can take time to remedy.

It is important to remember that guilt is a common reaction to loss, but it can ultimately be part of the healing process. However, if it is not addressed, excessive guilt can lead to psychological health concerns, such as depression, apathy, or generalized anxiety when survivors don't do the following:

- Acknowledge their feelings and recognize that they are part of a normal reaction to uncommon circumstances.
- Seek out other people for support to share their feelings, such as with a peer, friend, or family member, or join a support group to help them cope.

- Take time to mourn. Attend a religious or community ceremony, or plan their own way to remember the fellow service member, friend, or loved one.
- Turn feelings into positive action. Make a contribution, hold a fundraiser, give blood, or participate in any volunteer action that makes the survivor feel like they are serving the greater good.

When feelings of guilt accompany reactions to combat stress, they can also be a symptom of post-traumatic stress disorder if they continue for more than a month. If feelings of guilt continue for months or interfere with job performance or interaction with others, then it is important to seek professional help.

Survivor's guilt was first documented and discussed after the Holocaust. What became clear in the decades that followed is survivors' guilt is far more common than it was initially understood. Survivor's guilt was previously a diagnosis in the DSM, but it was removed, and it's now classified as a symptom of PTSD.

What makes survivor's guilt, especially complex is that the experience varies dramatically for each individual. Whether a person experiences survivor's guilt, its duration and its intensity all varies from person to person. But, the underlying feelings are similar: feeling guilty that they survived when someone else died, and feeling they do not deserve to live when another person did not.In some cases, this includes feeling they could have done more to save another person; in other cases, it is feeling guilty that another person died saving you.

Familiar circumstances of survivor's guilt:
- After surviving war
- Surviving an accident
- Surviving a natural disaster
- Surviving an act of violence

Some less-discussed circumstances that can trigger survivor's guilt are:
- Surviving an illness that is fatal for others
- After a fellow drug-user dies of an overdose
- When a parent dies from complications of childbirth
- After receiving a organ transplant
- After causing an accident in which others died
- Guilt for not being present at the time of an acci-

dent to potentially save the person who died

- When a child dies before a parent
- Death of a sibling, especially in the case of an illness

As with so many types of guilt that arise in grief, some survivor's guilt is rational and some isn't. There are circumstances in which their action (or lack of action) did impact the death of another. In these cases, there is a rational source of the guilt. In other cases, the guilt isn't tied to something a person did or didn't do. Instead, the person feels guilty about what they perceive they could or should have done. This guilt often defies logic, and is not rational.

Some theorists have suggested that this may be because people would prefer to blame themselves for things outside their control rather than to accept they are helpless.

Although survivor's guilt can have a lasting and significant impact on mental and emotional well-being if unaddressed, it may also serve an adaptive function. Those who survive may transform their feelings of guilt into a sense of increased meaning and purpose. They may also use survivor's guilt as a way to cope with the feelings of helplessness and powerlessness that can occur in traumatic situations. For some, survivor's guilt may also represent a connection to those who died, as feelings of guilt may keep the memories of the deceased alive, at least, for a time.

One significant thing to remember is, whether rational or irrational, survivor's guilt is normal. It is difficult to reconcile feeling grateful to be alive while knowing others did not share the same fate.

Further complicating general survivor's guilt is the fact that some survivors struggle with unresolved conflicts with the deceased. Survivors may feel a certain loss of hope knowing they were unable to make amends before the person's death.

Even if a survivor believes, somehow, they shouldn't still be here, they must remind themselves of who would be devastated if they were not alive. They must think of all the people who care deeply about them, and who are overjoyed and relieved they are okay. Survivors have been given the gift of survival, so, rather than rejecting that gift because they somehow feel undeserving, sharing it with those who love them is the very least they can do because those people deserve it.

Everyone thinks of things they would do differently if given another chance, but no one can change the past or predict the future. Many things that may seem clear now would have been impossible to predict at the time.

It's important not to get stuck on the why questions. When events like this happen, we often fixate on the why. If there is a why, we can't know what it is, no matter how long we obsess about it. Difficult as it is, try to let go of asking the why question, and focus on the meaning you can create from your survival. Whether it is big or small, seek the ways you will create something from this second chance.

CHAPTER 1

WOUNDED

The sound of the helicopter propellers as they whirred furiously seemed to signify a war drum or Bill's furiously beating heart. They were finally over the tiny forest where the militia had made their nest. Bill took a deep breath while uttering a prayer at the same time before blowing on the whistle, signaling to his men to jump in three seconds. "One, two, three!" And down in perfect synchronization, the men dived. Bill couldn't help the little smile of pride and honor for his country that flitted across his lips as he watched them go to fulfill one of the missions ordered by the commander and chief. Habitually displaying his paternal skill since he was the oldest soldier, he glanced over his shoulder into the chopper to ascertain that everyone had gotten off, and everything was in place. Then just as he turned towards the cockpit to let the pilot know he was going down, he saw a quick bright flash from the side of his eye. He turned sharply, lost his grip, and almost fell from the chopper.

He couldn't believe his eyes; the little patch of forest was engulfed in flames. He resisted the urge to panic, and immediately gave the command to the pilot to fly as low as possible. They had already been searching for survivors to rescue, but now, he feared some of the other medics had become victim's themselves. The enemy had made some improvised explosive devices because their recon group had extensively scanned the whole area for any nuclear weapons or combustibles. Suppressing the rage and fear in his mind, he managed not to tear at his flesh as he stared intently into the intentional flames of death, diligently searching for any of his men. The heat was unbearable, even from his perch at the mouth of the chopper, and he was about to call out to the pilot to swoop even lower when he heard something sharp whizz by his ear, and go through the side of the chopper. "*Bullets*!" The insurgents were shooting at them! "Take off, take off!" he roared at the pilot, fighting the urge to let out a wail.

He moved back into the empty interior of the chopper, and collapsed into a desolate heap on the floor in a position where he wasn't taunted with the fact that he had seen his fellow medics defeated, tortured, and destroyed by those intentional flames of death executed by the enemy.

Bill was seated upright on a bed in the medical hold tent. He didn't have any injuries on his body, but his mind was badly scarred. He had been back at the military base for the past five days. As a result, he hadn't been able to get up to even three hours of sleep without his conscience tormenting him with vivid pictures of the fire, and a raging inferno as he pulled all the men up one after the other, but he was powerless to help them. His legs wouldn't move, so all he could do was watch, and listen powerlessly as the men screamed out his name with arms stretched towards him to save them as they became engulfed by the flames. A stench of burning flames in his nostrils triggered a level of fear so deep within him that he let out a scream of guilt, and pain so intense that all the other soldiers became afraid.

A nurse had said something about his wife coming to pick him up. He had a 30-day leave, but he couldn't process everything that was said to him after all that had occurred. The flames were all he could think about. The name of each of his fellow soldiers rang in his head, and he'd shake his head as if to release some of his burdening thoughts.

Whenever he dozed off, he saw himself running in a maze with fire on all sides. His throat was dry and parched, and he could feel his lungs collapsing as he gasped desperately for air, but he couldn't give in. He mustn't pass out. The other soldiers were here in this maze. He could hear their voices. All of them called to him, and he was going to save them this time around if it was the last thing he did. But his throat was tightening... tightening... and then, his body became wracked with loud dry coughs, the type you imagine has blood spurting out. He was experiencing a sudden episode of anxiety with physical symptoms; it was a panic attack. The doctors kept him mildly sedated to keep him calm during transport.

In his mind, he was in a different environment where everything was white, and a soft hand was patting him softly, but consistently. Something about that hand felt familiar, but he couldn't pinpoint what, and then through his blurred vision, he saw a face he loved. It was his wife. "Hey honey," she said in the most natural voice. "I'm here now, and I'm taking you home."

Bill was in disbelief. He thought he was still in Iraq and could not comprehend how he had returned to the states.

"I'll take care of you," she said sweetly.

A team of nurses helped him get into a wheelchair and wheeled him outside to the parking lot where he eased into the passenger seat with a sense of relief. His wife reached over from the driver's seat and kissed him on his cheek as she reached across to help him with his seatbelt. She began to chatter randomly about their son and how excited he was about his dad coming home. According to the words coming from her mouth, he'd been quite the truant, throwing tantrums for the most unnecessary things. Bill wasn't paying any mind to her chatter, but he came to life when he heard her say, "Hopefully, your being at home will help calm him down, and maybe the two of you can have some quality father-son time."

"*Hopefully,*" he thought to himself dully, even though a bit of light seemed to have peeked out from all the darkness within for just a second. He felt compelled to say "hopefully" one more time, believing the traumatic event that had occurred would be an emotional burden consuming his daily thoughts during his leave of absence.

The thirty-day leave from Iraq seemed to be over before it even started, like a person who is off work for the weekend and can't believe it's Monday already.

After saying all his goodbyes and loading the car with luggage, Bill and his wife began riding back to the Fort McCoy Army base in Wisconsin. The time they spent together seemed to be like a fleeting moment as she desired for her husband to stay with her longer, but she knew his military duties were calling for him as they traveled along the road.

Then, like a block of ice suddenly falling from a tall building in the Chicago winter, shattering the fragile skull of someone walking below, leaving them blinded and disoriented, seemingly carelessly floating away in the brisk air…. There was one, two, three, then a pile-up of four trucks on top of the car transporting the soldier enroute to answer the summons of the Commander and Chief of the United States, and the woman he loved. Their bodies lay paralyzed and shattered by the weight of the vehicles.

Sirens blared one after the other as numerous police cars, fire trucks, and ambulances rushed to the scene of the accident. The first responders were surrounded; and almost blinded by a smoldering haze of thick black smoke as they weaved through a scorching maze of damaged metal, bypassing hundreds of flickering sparks that attempted to ignite into full flames. The air medical team helicopter transported his wife's injured body while the police escorted the paramedics on the ground as they transported the other victims at the speed of light, strategically moving through and around other vehicles on the road with ease and precision, as though there was a hand of safety on top of their vehicles guiding them.

They ran fiercely through the doors of the hospital emergency room wheeling in the stretchers one after the other into a crowd of doctors and nurses that were waiting. The wheels of IV poles and crash carts screeched as the medical assistants pushed them down the hallway, and the tones of hospital monitors and other medical equipment played a melody of life saving beats in the background, seemingly harmonizing with the male and female voices of the medical staff in conjunction with the beats of fingers and hands moving to the sound of sterilized medical instruments crashing against metal trays and vibrating like the sound cymbals.

The doctors informed the family that Bill's wife did not survive the impact of the accident. The loud outcry of family rage, pain, and tears repeatedly occurred through each phone call as they notified other family and friends of the tragic death and the questionable impending fate of Bill as he lay nearly lifeless in a coma.

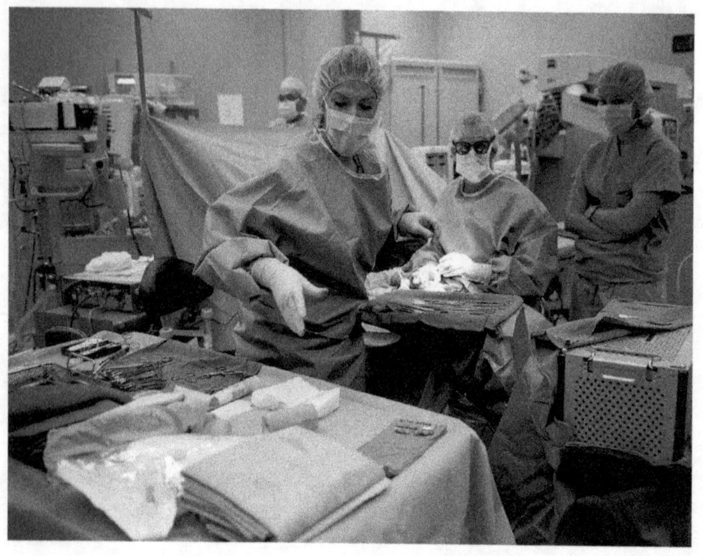

Over the course of several months, the doctors stated that Bill would not awake from the coma, and the best decision would be to disconnect life support. Due to the severe amount of brain injury he had suffered, even if he did wake up, he would be in a vegetative state for the rest of his life confined to an institution needing medical care around the clock.

Bill's resting body lay in the hospital bed like the deep still of the ocean with smooth, gentle calming rhythmic waves moving up and down while his spirit willingly traveled on a faraway journey…

He was walking around in a beautiful field with sunlight brighter than the human eye had ever seen, yet it was not blinding. He felt a loving type of calmness as the pleasant breeze brushed against him. He knew that he had never been there before, yet it was familiar and comfortable just like home.

"Hey, how are you doing?" He asked a girl walking by.

The girl never replied; she kept on moving. It was like she was right there in front of him, but he could not talk to her or even touch her. He tried to grab her, but each time, she would float away in the air. Finally, she looked at him, but then she turned away again. She kept walking toward a certain place, and Bill kept following. Somehow he knew that he wanted to go with her, although he had no idea where it was that she was going. After a while, he suddenly found himself standing in the doorway of the very hospital where he was lying in a coma. It was strange because up until then, he had forgotten about what happened to him earlier. He felt drawn to run in a certain direction and after a while, he got to the room where he was laying.

He saw his mom sobbing on the bed next to him, and his

father trying to console her. He felt something go through him, like an emotion when his mother touched his body in the bed. At first, he didn't know what to make of it; then, like a bolt of lightning, the idea struck him he could feel their every emotion. He moved closer to his body and looked at his face. He stared at his face for a while, but he didn't see a single movement, he did not even see a breath. He immediately felt like the world was shrinking; his chest felt constricted, and he found it difficult to breathe.

Just as all these things were happening; his mom and dad looked at each other. They were feeling an overwhelming emotion that was different from anything that they had felt before; it was more like helpless fear. Bill knew why they were feeling that way. It was because that was how he felt.

The doctors walked in the room to carry out some examinations, and his mother asked, "Please doctor, is there any more news or any new hope that he might wake up? He looks like…. He looks like he is dead."

The doctor sighed, and he was not sure what to tell her. "Nothing has changed. As I said before, even if he regained consciousness, the probability that he would still be able to remember anything or even speak is very low due to the permanent brain damage. He will just lay there for the rest of his life."

Another doctor said, "Ma'am, all the other injuries he has, the broken femur, cracked ribs, and all the rest would heal with time, all thanks to the fact that he had no permanent organ damage. However, the hard blow to his frontal cortex left permanent brain injury. He would have amnesia and the inability to use his body properly. He would be a body lying in a bed, not knowing anything."

Bill's mom burst into tears. However, Bill noticed that all this time, his dad had not said a single word apart from holding his mother close. He moved closer to his dad and tried holding his hand, even though his father could not feel anything. Bill could feel all the emotions that his father was trying to subdue. He could feel this overwhelming anger that his father was feeling, and it felt odd to him. "Why would he be angry?" He said to himself. Bills father had told others that he was asleep during the time the accident occurred. An image of Bill wearing all white had appeared to him and he asked Bill, "What are you doing here?" And why aren't you in Iraq?" Then the image of Bill faded away. His father received a phone call from the hospital informing him of the accident when he awoke.

Just then, the heart monitor alarm went off. His heart had stopped. The nurses came running, and they quickly pulled out the defibrillator. They were trying hard to start his heart again. As they applied the first shock to his body, Bill felt intense pain and everything he was looking at suddenly faded away.

Bill was pulled back to the beautiful field. However, now there were a lot of people around. From all the smiles on their faces, he could tell they were happy being there. It was almost as if he was in paradise. As he kept looking around, all he could feel was a complete joy. He could see vibrant colors, adults, children, teenagers and elders everywhere. He felt someone standing behind him, so he looked over his shoulder, and that was when he saw her. It was the girl again.

"Who are you?" He asked.

The girl smiled and replied, "I don't know, but you should know who I am. After all, I am here because you want me to meet you here."

Bill was surprised. He was sure that he had never seen this girl before, and he wondered how he could want someone that he had never seen before to be with him.

"Okay, if you don't know who you are, you should at least know where we are."
On hearing this, she ran into the field, laughing heartily and shouted, "You know where this is, and it is everything you have thought about for a very long time, wondering if it is real or not."

"Wait, are you saying this is heaven?" His eyes lit up like a candle as he said this.

The girl kept walking on as she talked, "It is not what you call it that matters. What you need to understand is that a place like this does exist."

He was confused. "So, where is this place exactly?"

She turned around and smiled. Her smile reminded him of something, and it also invoked peace within him.

"This is a place where all that exists is happiness, and none of the sadness of the heart exists here."

Bill nodded his head as he followed her around, looking at all that was in the beautiful field. It did look like everyone here was happy, but the problem he had was that it all seemed too good to be true, and also, the only way he had been told that anyone could get to heaven was to die. Since that was what he thought the place was, he wondered if they were dead. Suddenly, he stopped in his tracks and asked, "So, does this mean I am dead?"

The girl smiled and replied, "You are not dead, but you are not exactly alive at this moment either. You are in a state of higher consciousness. To your family, you are sleeping without waking up, and your body is seriously injured. It is possible that you might never wake up; The Highest Power will make that decision. But if you do, now you can be assured that there is a place for you to go where you can always be happy. Because if you awake, you will have quite a journey that will be filled with pain and trouble, you had to come here to revive or you would faint along the way."

Bill listened, but his vision of the words pain and trouble seem to be just vague images of words that he could see floating around him. He reached out, but could not grasp them, nor comprehend the meaning of them. It was like the words pain and trouble were present, but they meant nothing.

Bill had so many questions to ask, but he decided to keep them to himself. He was enjoying the surreal moment too much and wanted to stay. He moved on from place to place until it was night time. When anyone needed fire, all they had to do was speak it into existence. It was wonderful; he was intrigued by what he saw. It didn't matter who else was there, they all just seemed to be at peace with themselves.

They all gathered around the fire they had created and started telling stories about their time in another realm. Bill, at this point, figured the girl may not have been able to reveal that they were all dead. He didn't understand what was happening because some of them talked about all the things they wish to do differently when they go back to their lives. They all kept talking about themselves. When it was time for the girl to speak, she pointed at Bill and said, "He knows my story."

Bill was surprised; he was not sure how he was supposed to tell the story of someone he had just met. They all started cheering, "Bill! Bill! Bill!" She nudged him to stand up and tell her story. Bill stood up slowly and walked to the center of the circle they had formed. As he stood there, he heard her voice from behind him say, "Just believe!"

He began speaking, "Her name to me is little baby. Her body was born into a family of love and joy. She never knew any days of sadness, trials, and tribulations. She was loved in the womb, and everyone was waiting for her. She was what you would call the new hope for the family. She never had a chance to smile and laugh, but the hope of her life brought out the goodness in everyone. However, one day, while her family was gathered for a family reunion, there was great pain because she was born without life. That day took away so much from both her family and family friend's. The grief of her stillbirth was greatly over-whelming to me as a child. I did not know that someone so young could die, I thought only old people died. The talk of a baby's funeral terrified me. If young people died, then I might die too. I couldn't sleep for days because I was afraid that I might not wake up. The family's suffering, scared me so badly that I purposed in my mind to never think about it again and forget that it had ever happened."

He finished telling the story with tears rolled down his cheeks. Now, he understood when she said he wanted her there. It was because he was thinking about her subconsciously even though he never knew it. Everyone has an inner child deep inside them, hiding some unresolved issue that occurred during childhood. As the years moved on, he had stopped thinking about it consciously, but it was still there.

Now he remembered, he touched her face and smiled amidst the tears he was shedding and asked, "Why were you born not alive just to cause everyone so much pain and crying? Why were you even born? They needed you to be happy."

The girl cleaned his tears and kissed him on the cheek.

"All of you had all you needed." She said, "Always remember, everything that happens where you reside is always connected to someone in another realm. They all wanted me, but I was needed here. I just made an appearance to give them a glimpse of their wants, and so they would know one day they would have what they wanted. I'm okay here." I need to give you the assurance of knowing that your strength and treasures are here just a prayer away when you need them.

Bill looked around at all the people in the beautiful field. He could see that everyone was happy, and it all made him even angrier. He wondered why he lived in a world where he felt angry every day, and there were people here just being happy and living a good life. He looked around, and there were no policemen. The air smelled fresh, and even elderly people were thriving with resilience. He kept on walking. He ran for a while and then he jogged. He was looking to see if he was going to find something bad happening somewhere, but everywhere seemed so peaceful that he was sure this place did not exist. The fact that he was unsure if he was dead or not made him even more confused about everything. He screamed out at the top of his lungs, "Is this real?... Never mind, this is just a hallucination, and it will all be over when I wake up."

As he journeyed back through some of the past times in his life, he was not sure why everything seemed so unfamiliar.

"Do you know why things seem so unfamiliar? It is because you chose to forget, said the girl." She began showing him many events that occurred during his lifetime, he felt a sense of gentle peace from the burden of fear, regret, and unhappiness. He laid down, resting in the beautiful field until he heard someone call his name. He opened his eyes, sat up, and began looking around to see who had called him.

At the hospital, the music therapy department musicians were playing a song right outside of Bill's door, while the priest was inside the room comforting the family. With a Bible in his hand, he was reading somber scripture verses that would console someone experiencing a loss.
While everyone was pondering over whether or not to disconnect life support and allow him to transition from earth, Bill began to experience an extreme amount of brain activity. The doctors rushed into the room to read the monitors and examine him. Then suddenly, like the sun

rising to its full position and shining at its brightest and providing illumination to conquer the darkness, he opened his eyes and spoke for the first time in several months. He was met with flashlights probing at his eyes and he felt like a feather being lifted off the ground by the wind as he was being raised to a sitting position by the staff. The doctors had said that it would be nearly medically impossible for him to wake up after all that time, but that was exactly what happened. He awoke.

When Jesus came into the official's house and saw the flute-players and the crowd in noisy disorder, He said, "Leave; for the girl has not died, but is asleep." And they began laughing at Him. But when the crowd had been sent out, He entered and took her by the hand, and the girl got up.

Matthew 9: 23-25 (NASB)

CHAPTER 2
LIVING AGAIN

After a year long out-of-state hospital stay, Bill was finally able to say goodbye to the doctors who repeatedly said he would never wake up. He looked directly into their eyes as a gesture to show them that he was wide awake. The brain controls the coordination of the leg muscles, which make it possible for a person to walk. Bill walked out with slow, fragmented steps and waved while smiling at one particular medically intelligent nurse that discouraged him daily by telling him to stop attempting to get out the bed because he would never walk again.

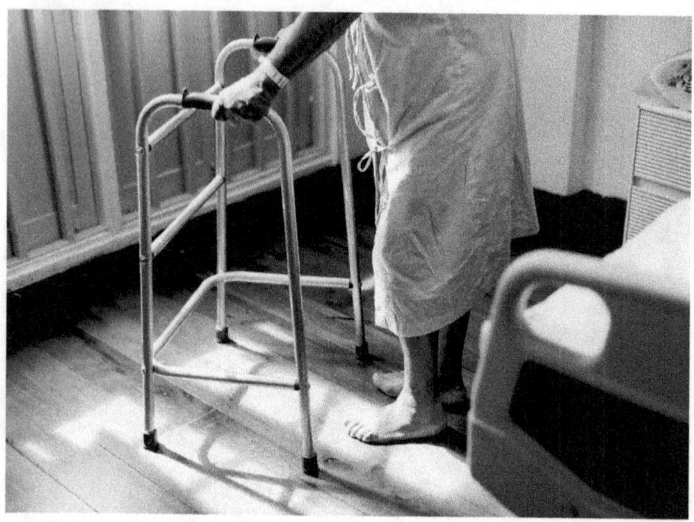

He was discharged into the care of his family with many years of rehabilitation ahead of him without his spouse and the responsibility of a young child. They had taken over his finances for the year that he was incapacitated. After all the events related to the accident, there was nearly a half million dollars that rightfully belonged to Bill and his young son that was missing. Bill confronted his family members concerning the inconsistencies in the accounts, to which they blatantly denied any wrongdoing whatsoever. In their defense, they claimed the expense of constantly traveling out-of-state to visit him and the funeral for his wife had depleted his funds. Bill was hospitalized and not able to attend the funeral.

But even with taking those matters into consideration, there was still a huge financial discrepancy that resulted in a commotion that escalated until he and his son was forced out of the house by his family members. Being low on cash and rendered homeless by his family, he had to take up shelter with his son in a car. It was a very trying time for him and his son, as Bill was in the midst of physical therapy and was still learning how to walk again.

The matriarch of the family had passed away a few years earlier. Without the elders around who held the reins on the family, anything was bound to happen. The family believed the doctor's report that said even if Bill awoke from the coma, he would be so mentally deficient that he would never be able to hold an intelligent conversation. Thus, he would never know that his finances had been squandered.

His anger grew when he learned they had purchased three-flat buildings, new cars, jewelry, exotic vacations and other expensive items all paid in cash, yet there was nothing set aside for him nor for his young son. His spouse was an extravagant woman, and nobody seemed to know what happened to all of her fur coats, jewelry, fine art, designer clothing, and a safe full of cash savings with more than enough to live off for a couple of years.

Then, with the help of a Department of Veteran Affairs advocate, he was able to sublease a condominium, from a family friend, after the VA expedited his disability payments. He was a good tenant that paid his rent faithfully on time each month. It felt like a true blessing to be in a stable residence of his own while he tried to re-establish his life. But, a year later, he learned the condo owner had not been paying the assessment fees. Once again, he was evicted; all his belongings and furniture had been damaged or destroyed from sitting outside on the sidewalk during inclement weather.

Many psychiatrists have often stated that money and possessions have always been two of the most intense emotional subjects to mankind. Being placed in a situation where the very assets needed to thrive in life have been morally or wrongfully taken away, then to have your intelligence (which is not lacking, just cognitively slow) insulted with lies and deception, is enough to cause a reasonable thinking person to exhibit the type of damaging rage that could cause physical harm. Not to mention provoking a war time veteran that has the experience of battlefield violence, death, and destruction lying dormant in the memories of their mind with the potential to flare up and cause someone to become a battlefield victim of their temporary displaced reality, but Bill remained subdued.

He suppressed the severity of his physical and emotional pain so he would not appear to be a burden. Instead, he focused on managing and appeasing his family's ongoing imaginary offense for being questioned about his missing money, and their daily signifying gestures that were intended to intimidate and discourage him from speaking about the subject of his money.

Being in a state of lack, want, and constantly desiring independence can often cause people to develop a sense of low self-esteem. This can become a debilitating condition that some people are never able to recover from during their entire life once they develop a consciousness of poverty within themselves. That was the only time in his adult life that he was not 100% functional and independent. Even as a young man during his college years, he traveled from out- of- state back to his hometown on the weekends to work at a part-time job. But now, his hand trembling fear was evident to him, and he often felt alone while facing a big mean world with a brain that was no longer capable of processing the complications and difficulties of life before they had the opportunity to overtake and damage him in some way. There was always a constant inner conflict between the desire of independence and his mind whispering condemnation for past life mistakes, invoking guilt for the gift of his very life after others that he perceived to be more worthy of living had perished. In reality, nobody ever knows the full depth of the secret sins that hide within the heart of another person. The mental game of overlooking wrongdoing and allowing others to take advantage of his situation continued for years.

Even while wearing an emotional bullet proof vest there was often a need to run, hide and dodge the attack of verbal bullets, the kind that have been known to pierce the spirit, causing so much internal damage that hope, dreams and desires begin to die a slow lingering death until the day there is no more life within them. Playing the timid male game during that time seemed to be the only way to defeat the fear of being isolated and left to face the world alone as the reality of being home became real. In the blink of an eye, he had gone to sleep then awoke from the coma into the reality that he was no longer the man of honor who once received admiration and respect from the troops for his strength and courage. He was now a vulnerable fragment of his former self.

When his veteran disability benefits were approved, they included the ability for the VA to make monthly rental payments to a family member or friend if Bill desired to reside at their home, instead of living on his own. That was in addition to nearly two thousand dollars a month to assist Bill with activities of daily living, along with free health and dental coverage. Suddenly, friends and family offered to assist when they became aware of the government benefits they could receive due to Bill's military disability status, and those who were not able to gain any benefit from his disability withdrew their assistance. That revealed the true nature of their heart, there was a simulated show of concern as long as the condition was met to provide some benefit for them in return, quid pro quo. There was never an equally comparable ongoing concern with the same level of intense caring and emotional shielding from the negative impact that their unnecessary stress, strife and railing had on Bill's traumatic brain injury. Every overly dramatic stressful event since the accident has been a result of the various displays of angry behavior by family or friends, with the intent to manipulate or harass Bill into providing some form of financial benefit for them.

He often states that family is always counting his money in their minds and asking him to justify how he spends the money that he earns. And he wonders, do church folks actually believe, act, and live by the guilt cliches that they often say to him? "money ain't everything" "whatever happened, that's your family" "you only got one mama and daddy" "let the Lord handle it" "the Lord giveth and the Lord taketh away."

Traumatic Brain Injury is a lifelong condition that must always be acknowledged regardless of the fact that the physical disability cannot be seen like someone in a wheelchair or a deformed person. The depth of its severity can reveal itself many years after the injury, such as in the Whalen case where a Colorado man was hit in the head with a baseball bat, endured being in a coma then awoke and resumed his life. But eight years later, without suffering any further injuries or additional medical problems, he was found dead in his bed at home. The coroner determined that the TBI he suffered was the cause of death. The case received national attention because the man who caused the injury had already been sentenced, therefore, when Whalen died several years later 'double jeopardy' prevented him from being charged with murder.

Neurologists have stated that undue stress can have a negative impact on a healthy brain. But for someone that has traumatic brain injury severe enough to result in a low score on the Glascow Coma Scale, the negative neurological impact on their damaged brain can be detrimental to their long-term, ongoing recovery. Although the symptoms may not show immediately, later in life the effects will begin to show physically through their neurological behavior. But the contribution to the destruction of Bill's neurological health from unnecessary stress has always been secondary and insignificant to those imposing the stress, since their motives are driven by greed and selfishness.

The strong determination that dwelled deep within Bill's heart assured him that his situation would not overtake and defeat him. He persevered daily with the assurance that someday, he would be restored to the life that he desired, despite the disappointing lack of faith and distorted life vision that the doctors and his family had for him. Every person that lives on the street is not broke and ignorant, there are homeless people that have extraordinary backgrounds and have people that are willing to assist them, but they lost hope and gave up on life after some devastating event. When Bill was forced out of his family's house and lived in his car he could have easily become another homeless veteran, if he had not desired to draw strength from the divine impartation of power to overcome his circumstances.

My enemies say of me in malice, "When will he die, and his name perish?" When one of them comes to see me, he speaks falsely, while his heart gathers slander; then he goes out and spreads it around. All my enemies whisper togeth-

er against me; they imagine the worst for me, saying, "A vile disease has afflicted him; he will never get up from the place where he lies." Even my close friend, someone I trusted, one who shared my bread, has turned against me. But may you have mercy on me, LORD; raise me up, that I may repay them.

Psalms 41: 5-11 (NIV)

"They saw him afar off, and before he came near to them, they conspired against him to kill him. They said one to another, "Behold, this DREAMER comes. Come now, therefore, and let's kill him, and cast him into one of the pits, and we will say, 'An evil animal has devoured him.' We will see what will become of his DREAMS."

"It happened, when Joseph came to his brothers, that they stripped Joseph of his coat, the coat of many colors that was on him; and they took him, and threw him into the pit..."

Genesis 37: 18-20and23-24 (WEB)

"Avoiding strife brings a man honor; only fools continue to argue."

Proverbs 20:3 (NEV)

*"Bread gained by deceit tastes sweet to a person, but after-
ward his mouth will be filled with gravel."*
Proverbs 20:17 (NET BIBLE)

CHAPTER 3
LOVE REUNION

As a part of ongoing therapy for the memory loss related to Bills traumatic brain injury (TBI), he would look at old photos to see how much he could remember from the past. As he flipped through several pages of old girlfriends in one of his photo albums, he ran across a twenty-five-year-old picture of a woman in a white outfit. There was an overwhelming feeling of happiness and peace when he looked at her picture, and he desired to find her. He couldn't remember her name, didn't know where she lived and he didn't remember anything specific about her, but there was one thing that was evident by the way he felt in his heart. In the past, he must have been in love with her and he had a burning desire to find her.

Although he was already involved in a relationship, he had become dissatisfied and attempted to dissolve the relationship several times. But the woman constantly reminded him of the care she provided during the early stages of his recovery, disregarding the fact she had been paid to provide the care, which made him feel obligated, so he decided to stay in the relationship each and every time he wanted to leave.

He kept the picture of the woman in his wallet for months showing it to people he ran into from his past asking them if they knew her and where she might live. He lit candles at the church and prayed that he would find her. About a year later, Bill was invited to a party by one of his old friends who had worked with him a long time ago, before his accident, and now she was retiring. He walked in through the main entrance slowly, taking his time to observe each face; he seemed to vaguely recognize some of them. He was still looking around for the familiar face of the host when he noticed a woman standing all alone by the punch bowl. The therapist had told him that actually being in the presence of a familiar face might help retrieve information from his memory.

This was one of those moments the therapist had talked about. It was the same woman in the picture that he had been carrying in his wallet for all those months. He had some vague flashbacks, but no matter how much he tried, at that moment, he could not recall her name. He stood transfixed in one spot, lost in thought, and desperately grasping at possible thoughts, hoping they would bring some answers to the puzzle he was trying to solve.

"Oh my God!" The woman at the punch bowl screamed out in excitement, as she rushed over to where Bill was still standing.

"I can't believe it. Is it you?" Tiffany asked as she hugged Bill.

"Yes, I suppose," Bill answered in a voice of hazy awe.

"I can't believe it; it's you. It's been a long time." Tiffany said.

Bill stared at her looking a bit embarrassed because he could not recall her name. He remembered the therapist's advice about asking questions whenever he was unsure, so he summoned the courage and finally spoke out.
"I know your face, but what is your name?" Bill asked.

"How's your wife?" Tiffany asked, interrupting him halfway into his sentence.

"My wife? My wife?" Bill asked with a stutter. "My wife was killed in a car accident. And I ended up in a coma for several months."

"Oh my God, I had no idea. I'm so sorry," Tiffany exclaimed.

"Thank you, but like I was trying to let you know, I'm having trouble remembering many things, so please remind me of your name." Bill said.

"Well, how do I say this? Emm." Tiffany paused for a while, looked up at Bill, and then smiled again before continuing. "My name is Tiffany. Do you remember that we dated a long while ago?" She finished off with a smile before taking a sip of punch.

Bill smiled the entire time that he was in her presence, the palpable energy of love and happiness he could sense as he spoke with her was surreal to him. After processing the information he had just received, he began to wonder what happened to their old relationship. The relationship must have ended. Otherwise, he would not have married someone else. He had always been what some called a charming 'ladies man' so maybe that was the reason.

"If you don't mind me asking, what happened to us?" Bill insisted on an answer as he gestured at himself and Tiffany with his hands.

"It will all come back to you one day," Tiffany said with a reassuring pat on Bill's shoulder.

Tiffany smiled again. Smiling came easily to her. Bill could see why he would have fallen in love with her.

"Wow, I have trouble remembering a lot of things," Bill replied with a deep sigh.

"Don't worry, that will get better," Tiffany said with a reassuring smile.

"I feel like there's a lot for us to talk about, that's if you don't mind," Bill said.

"No problem. It'll be my pleasure," Tiffany said.

"Give me a second then. I need to say a quick hello to the host." Bill said.

It seemed coincidental that after all these years, they should meet again. Fate surely had a funny way of playing out. Now that they had met each other again, it was only fair to catch up with the events of their lives.

Bill walked up to Tiffany; this time, he was the first to smile.

"We should get some place to sit. I usually don't like standing for long since the accident," Bill said, pausing to take a sip from the can of root beer he was now holding." Follow me. I spotted some vacant chairs out back," he continued, as he pointed in the direction he had just returned from.

"No problem. But first, let me get you a plate of food. Do you still like chicken wings?" Tiffany asked as they both headed in the direction of the food.

"Some things never change," Bill chuckled in reply.

Tiffany served him a plate with a good helping of chicken wings. She got an extra plate for herself and two more drinks. They both sat down and placed their plates of food on a nearby table.

The host of the party was a former colleague of both Bill and Tiffany a long time ago.

"I see that you've found each other," Another former collegue said as she walked up to the couple seated at the table.

"Yeah, we have," Tiffany replied as their old collegue pulled up a seat for herself.

"How time flies, huh?" Their old collegue said before pausing to stare at Bill and Tiffany.

"You know, working those damn shifts wondering when I was going to get off work, and go back home became a vicious cycle: home, work, and home then back to work again. Now, I'm retired and do just as much work."

"The irony of life," Tiffany added jokingly before continuing. "You'll be surprised at the amount of work there is to do at home".
They all burst out in laughter at Tiffany's comment.

"It's really good to see you guys, especially like this. You know, I always fancied the two of you as a great couple. You guys seemed inseparable back in the day."

"Like they say, things just happen," Tiffany said with a coy smile.

"Yeah, it does happen. Like what happened to you," Their old collegue said as she looked in Bill's direction. "It was an unfortunate event, losing your wife in that accident. You've been through a whole lot Bill, and I must salute your resilience. But you know what? The worst is behind you already, you're doing fine, and whatever mistakes of the past can always be corrected."

"Thanks, "Bill said with a sincere look of appreciation.

"How's your son? He's already a grown man by now." Their old collegue said.

"He's doing fine. He should be back from college any day." Bill said.
"My regards to him." Their old collegue said.

"We'll be talking," Bill and Tiffany said as they walked away from their table.

Over the next few hours, Bill and Tiffany talked only pausing to get a refill of their drinks. They felt like two souls who had just gotten back together after a separation. They had so much to talk about. The events of more than twenty-five years could not be covered in just one sitting, especially with the emotional trials and struggles Bill had endured since his accident. Although, Tiffany had lived a relatively happy life in comparison, she still had her life troubles like every average mid-lifer.

"I need to walk around for a bit; sitting for too long always makes my knees stiff," Bill told Tiffany.

"No problem, we can walk around. Being sedentary for too long isn't good, but if you elevate your leg, it will help prevent swelling," Tiffany said.

"Seems like you're taking care of me already, and it's barely been a few hours since we met up again," Bill replied.

"A toast, to finding long lost love and to a brighter future," Bill said as he raised his glass to toast finally finding Tiffany.

From that day forward, they rode on the storms of life together as they faced many trials and strong opposition from family, friends and former love interests after Bill decided to have a wife again.

When family and friends have become comfortable with your living situation and have placed themselves in a position to benefit from the resources in your life, there will always be strong conflict when you make a change.

While employment bullying, harassment and creating hostile environments are illegal, it continues to run rampant within some families. A genuine loving concern for someone will always cause an individual to realize that their feelings and desires should be insignificant when it is causing a negative impact on the wellbeing of another, especially when the person the behavior is being directed toward is not obligated to provide anything to them in life.

Even several years later, former family neighbors reminded Bill of how his family had flaunted their new found fortune while he was hospitalized. But, he continued to remain focused on the blessings that God showered upon him, while his family continued to pretend like they never financially benefited from the trauma that he suffered, as if the passing of time should make their past actions unimportant and forgettable.

Tiffany became a strong emotional pillar that Bill was able to lean upon. Their enduring love was stronger than the attacks of their adversaries. A couple of years later, Bill and Tiffany married.

"He that finds a wife finds a good thing, and receives the will of Lord Jehovah, and he that puts away a good wife puts away good from his house."
Proverbs 18:22 (ARAMIC Bible in plain English)

"In the same way, you husbands must live with your wives with the proper understanding that they are more delicate than you. Treat them with respect, because they also will receive, together with you, God's gift of life. Do this so that nothing will interfere with your prayers."
1 Peter 3:7 (GNT)

CHAPTER 4

DESTINY

The accident that wounded Bill, leaving him with traumatic brain injury (TBI) and causing him to become a widower was in January of 2006. One day, Tiffany was looking back in a old prayer journal that she kept and noticed that on New Year's Day in 2006, she wrote, "Lord, I desire a husband. I don't know who you will let find this good thing to be their wife, but wherever they are get them prepared for me as you get me prepared for them." A few days later, one of her very best friends died and the heartfelt agony of no longer having a close confidant to discuss the issues of life with anymore intensified the desire for her prayer to be answered. She disliked driving and often took the bus to the mall. At one of the stoplights along the route, she would often look and admire the houses in a particular subdivision, visualizing herself opening the door and being greeted by a small dog. The times she did drive, it was her favorite make of car. When Bill and Tiffany first dated over twenty-five years ago, he was a fast food restaurant manager and she was a factory worker. Nearly three decades later, when they reunited, Bill was a disabled veteran and Tiffany had become a nurse at the urging of all the caregivers in her family, as she did not have any interest in the medical field. Bill was living with a family member while searching for a home of his own when they reunited. Tiffany had never mentioned any particular area where she liked the homes, but when Bill chose the home he wanted to purchase, to her surprise, it was in the very area she had visualized several years earlier when she looked on from the bus stop. They reside there today. Bill drove a nice truck, then without Tiffany having any knowledge, one day he came to pick her up in a new car that he had purchased. It just happened to be her favorite make of car. They worked on different shifts and often Tiffany told Bill that she was lonely while he was at work.

One day, he came home surprising her with a small dog to keep her company. Tiffany was sitting on the bench at the mall one day thinking about the future and wondering who she should share her life with; she put money into a vending machine to purchase a drink. A cola company had launched a personal name campaign at that time. The writing on the bottle of cola that was dispensed said: "share a coke with William" (Bill's full name).

SHARE A Coke WITH
William

The doctors had already given up on Bill after being involved in the accident that left him with permanent traumatic brain injury and on life support in the hospital for a long time. All hope seemed to be lost as the doctor advised Bill's family to "pull the plug," and let go.

Remember Job in the Bible? He lost virtually everything and was helpless as he watched the life draining out of him. His wife and friends, who should have been sympathetic about losing him, simply advised him to curse God and die. Not because they would not miss him, and not because they were heartless, but because then, having him dead seemed to be the best option. They thought to have him alive in such pain, disgrace and embarrassment from his diminished health and wealth was pointless. But, not only was Job healed, but God also restored everything he had lost two fold (Job 42:10).

Also, like Job, Bill didn't give up in his spirit while appearing to be in a deep sleep to others. He not only woke up, but he has made great progress in his recovery. Despite being a disabled Army Veteran with permanent traumatic brain injury (TBI), memory loss, grief from the loss of a spouse and fellow soldiers, overcoming survivor's guilt and family betrayal, he started to live, find love and enjoy life again.

His long-time employer modified his job after his injury, which allowed him to continue working; he can walk with support, drive a vehicle utilizing directions as needed, complete activities of daily living with directions and owns a home of his own. Bill found love again when he was reunited with a woman (Tiffany) he had known nearly three decades before his ordeal.

Whenever you get to a point where it appears that all hope is gone, in your moments of despair, keep the faith. There is light at the end of that tunnel. Do not become afraid, give up, or lose hope when you see a bend in the road, for it is not the end of the road. Keep believing, because God is too faithful to fail you. If he didn't fail Job, gave Bill a new start and answered Tiffany's prayer after several years of waiting with someone from her past that she no longer consciously thought about anymore, then he can do the same for you.

Remember, Bill and Tiffany dated and then separated

many years ago, and all the events that occurred over the years in their lives played a role in their future destiny. If Bill had not left the fast food industry to accept a county job then he may have been terminated like many other veterans after they became injured, and if he had not joined the military he would not have become a disabled veteran, and if he hadn't served during a war in progress when President Obama's term began, then he would not have received all the military benefits that were implemented for Iraq soldiers.

And if his employer wasn't willing to modify his job to accommodate his disability then he would not have been able to maintain his position. And if he hadn't lost his spouse and become uneasy and discontent with other love interest, then he would not have sought out a new love. And if Tiffany did not give him a picture of herself years earlier that he kept in his photo album, the doctors stated that without seeing the picture to remind him of their love all memory of her would have probably been forgotten due to the memory loss from his traumatic brain injury (TBI). And if Bill didn't have a strong longing desire to find Tiffany and if she didn't still have love in her heart for Bill, then his former love interest would have been able to destroy their relationship just as they destroyed all other love relationships Bill attempted to enter with other women. And if Tiffany didn't have a heartfelt desire for a husband that she wrote down in her prayer journal, then Bill may not have been seeking to find her. And if Bill hadn't become disabled then he may not need a nurse to care for him. And if Tiffany hadn't become a nurse then she may not understand the difficulties that Bill will face medically and emotionally for the rest of his life.

And if she didn't have a vision of a home with a little dog, then Bill may have never been led to purchase a home in a certain area and buy a dog for her. Destiny is a matter of choice, not a matter of chance. They both decided to accept and live in their divine ordained destiny. Sometimes, Tiffany wakes up in the middle of the night because Bill is poking on her, he always says "I just want to make sure this is real, I really have my Tiffany with me."

The events in life that appear to be a tragedy or accidental in our perception all have a divine plan. Bill and Tiffany consider it to be a blessing that they were able to under-stand the unfolding of events in their lives during this lifetime, as some issues cannot be understood until another lifetime. In their case, the long, difficult journey through an unforeseeable turn of events propelled them into their intended destination. Love reunited was their destiny.

For I know the plans I have for you," declares the LORD, "plans to prosper you and not harm you, plans to give you hope and a future.

Jeremiah 29:11 (NIV)

And we know that all things work together for good to them that love God, to them who are the called according to his purpose

Romans 8:28 (KJV)

CHAPTER 5

MANIFESTING LOVE

The Law of Attraction is a law, so it must happen. Just as we are aware that the law of gravity exists and we see it do its job every day of our lives, it does not make any difference whether you are sinner, saint, Muslim, Christian or a Jewish person, if you jump from the top of a high rise building the law of gravity is absolutely without fail going to take you down. The religious beliefs that you may have will not defy the law. Although it can be temporarily modified such as to fly an airplane, gravity is needed for the airplane to land. The

Law of Attraction does its job every day and it is completely your responsibility to alter the direction of the law so that it works in your favor rather than being a victim of whatever happens to you in life. The destinations in your life are your responsibility; the path you must take to reach your destination is controlled by the Universe.

If you choose to lift the veil and open your eyes to see how it works, then you will see it. However, if you choose otherwise, you will never know how the power within you can change your way of life and change it to the way you want it to be. Stop thinking that sounds too good to be true.

Let me give you examples, people who have attained success, wealth, and abundance in their lives with the help of the Law of Attraction. Andrew Carnegie was the wealthiest man in his time, he was the man who made his fortune in the steel industry and eventually became the richest in the world.

Many people do not know that Andrew Carnegie attained success using the Law of Attraction. He was able to live his dreams because he believed in himself, he had a burning desire towards attaining the success that he eventually achieved, and he was always willing to learn even though he had attained the title of being the wealthiest man on earth.

Henry Ford and Andrew Carnegie both knew the secret to be able to achieve or attain what they wanted in life. They were members of a brotherhood which taught them how to correctly use the Law of Attraction and they only shared that information with each other.

Using your mind to attract what you want isn't easy, which is where the old saying comes from that "it is easier to lift a building than to use your mind." But the mind is effective for the purpose of having your brain send vibrational frequencies out into the universe, which in turn gives back to you in the form of a physical manifestation.

Even though Andrew Carnegie, Henry Ford, and their likes have achieved something that most people are working hard to achieve, the fact remains that those people are human beings.

We all have thoughts, desires, and feelings, but what separates those people from ordinary people is their perspective. They knew that the principles of the Law of Attraction must be rigorously followed for it to able to work the way they wanted.

The information on how to use the law of attraction was only shared among those in secret societies in the old days, when a book was going to be published in the the 1950's making the information available to the public there was a major uproar and much of the information was altered. While the Bible contained the same principles, it was a tool that was used in religion for punishment and human restraint, not for success.

The objective is for you to become proficient in those principles so that you can achieve what other successful people have accomplished in life, their desires. It is absolutely necessary for you to be aware that you can be, have or do any and everything that you want as long as it is in alignment with the law and does not infringe on the rights of others or it will come back to harm you.

The US President Donald Trump has stated that success is genetic and it is passed down in the bloodline, examine that statement. Everyone is aware that certain diseases are genetic, but many people fail to think about why they may have been told that they act or look like a certain family member that they have never met or that may have passed away before they were born.

Scientist have studied and documented Genetic Memory for many years and state that individuals can inherit the experience of their ancestors that has been passed down through DNA. The problem is that many people have ancestors that have been devastated, overcome or defeated in life by the experience of poverty, slavery, failure, divorce or any other type of life altering experiences. Those who have inherited the effect of negative experiences have them playing in the background of their DNA, somewhat like a radio playing on low volume in the workplace.

Although a person may not consciously listen to the music because they are hard at work, at times they may find themselves tapping their foot or shaking their head without even realizing the music is having an effect on them. Most people do not hear music, and then consciously say to themselves "I'm going to pat my foot or shake my head to the beat." They just respond without any focused effort.

Have you ever known a family that has one child that chooses to go down a completely different path in life which may be positive or negative although they were raised in the same home with their siblings? And what about those who worked hard until the day they are lowered down into the grave, but they had never achieved success in life, while others seem to obtain their desires with little effort? Do you believe that they were just blessed, lucky or favored while other hard-working good-hearted people did not deserve to reach their goals? It is the unconscious programming in the subconscious that must be changed, and if it is not changed, then it won't matter how many new and different ways are tried to reach a goal, the end result will still be the same. In other words, it will be just like wheels spinning in place on a car without moving.

Important Note:

The law of attraction will be working to your disadvantage rather than to your advantage if you are not in alignment with what you desire. Remember the Law of Attraction is always happening. The LOA matches your energy, it mirrors back what you're sending out, whether you are purposefully attracting or stuck on a default setting like the majority of people.

Misalignment with what you desire will causes uncertainty,

doubt, anxiety, self-consciousness, and low self-esteem. Deep within yourself it feels like you are not very confident that your desires will be fulfilled, even if you are saying it with your mouth. The feeling of unpreparedness, not being good enough, smart enough, rich enough, thin enough, etc. is often the result of negative subconscious programming or negative DNA inheritance.

Being in harmony with your desire is the aspect of believing. Once the believing is present then you just have to connect with the object of your desire. Using the Law of Attraction for love and relationships works whether you believe it will or not.

Many people describe the law of attraction as the process by which thoughts become things. But mostly the process has more to do with energy dynamics. It's about becoming conscious of your internal state, attuning to your energy and using the connecting feeling to create your reality.

In other words, some people might say that your prayers are answered when you pray and feel a chill/tingling come over you. The key is to stay in that alignment. Please don't confuse human emotions with spiritual feelings, many church people have been told repeatedly and don't understand the meaning of the saying that "you cannot go by your feelings."

When using the law of attraction in relationships, you have to stop focusing on what your love life or relationships are like now.

If you think that you'll never find love, then that energy will cause the law of attraction to bring you more instances where you don't have love.

If you keep sowing all your energy into bad relationships then you will keep reaping back more bad relationships. The law of attraction is not Witchcraft, you can not use it to make someone fall in love with you against their will.

Don't look at your relationship as it is now, but visualize it and mentally picture how you want it to be. Live as if it already is a reality because many couples want to make their relationship work.

You can do various things to try to improve your relationship, but if they are carried out when you feel frustrated, angry, sad, or disappointed, you will not send the right type of vibration to attract improvement. You will send the vibration of frustration, anger, sadness, or disappointment.

When you use the Law of Attraction to fulfill your desires, you need to match your vibration with the frequency that you want to receive. Therefore, if you want your partner to be understanding and thoughtful, you need to be and feel understanding and thoughtful. That's why your frequency is important.

You can use attraction to turn things around and enhance your relationship. The best way to begin is to do the opposite of what you are probably doing right now that is not working. Don't pay attention to what your partner is doing that you dislike. Instead, focus intently on what you do like and what is going well between you.

Most couples start their relationships thinking positive, optimistic thoughts that are forgiving and kind toward each other. Later, expectations and responsibilities enter their union and baggage accumulates. When it does, negative thoughts creep into the picture, and people send negative vibrations to one another. As a result, they attract unhappiness.

Your feelings stem from your thoughts, which influence your perception regarding your relationship.

The process of manifesting gets easier with time and practice.

Attraction can bring you and your partner together. All you need to do to make your relationship work is to focus on joy and connectedness.

In my experience, the Law of Attraction is more simple than easy. The principle is incredibly simple: like attracts like, so believe in what you want and you will attract it into your life. Practicing the Law of Attraction is a little more complicated. The reason it is complicated is that you have to make a habit of practicing it. You don't do it once and see changes overnight. However, you can do it consistently and see changes over time for the rest of your life.

Using the Law of Attraction involves a process of visualizing your desires as already being in your possession. You believe that you already have the loving relationship you desire. You spend time experiencing the joy you imagine having in that relationship. You derive happiness from that relationship even though it doesn't exist in your actual physical reality.

Most people have noticed that once they enter into a relationship then suddenly other people are drawn to them, but when they were single they had the hardest time on earth finding a compatible mate. It's the same energy principle as with financially wealthy people who always draw more money to them, and people with a poverty consciousness always gain a nickle then have to spend a dime.

By experiencing positive feelings about yourself and the things you want, you align yourself with energies in the universe that operate on similar frequencies. You do so because you are operating on the same, more positive frequencies. The most important factor is believing in the potential reality of your dreams and desires. You can start enjoying the positive feelings associated with those things before you even have them. You just have to stay motivated and practice.

The attraction process as outlined here consists of 6 specific steps:

- Good feelings
- Decide on your intensions
- Act on opportunities and put something into ac-

tion
- Don't be concerned with "How"
- Open your heart and mind
- Allow the manifestation of the intention

Understanding the Law of Attraction is pretty simple. Consider that all manifestation begins with feelings. If you are feeling good, you will attract what you want. If you are feeling bad, you will attract what you do NOT want... period. Your state of being attracts everything to you.

You cannot attract wealth and success if you are feeling and speaking poorly, it takes a conscious effort NOT to join your peers who are making statements like:

"my money is funny"

"my change is strange"

"I would but I just ain't able"

"I have to rob Peter to pay Paul"

"I'm always a day late and a dollar short"

"I just can't get a break"

"I make two steps forward then three steps backward"

"If it wasn't for bad luck, I wouldn't have any luck"

"It's always something"

"I can't afford it"

You cannot attract health if you are feeling and speaking sickness. It takes a conscious effort NOT to feel and speak sickness statements like:

"I'm sick as a dog"
"this pain is killing me"

You cannot attract love if you don't feel worth. It takes a conscious effort NOT to feel and speak unworthy statements like:

"why don't they want me?"
"I wish I was taller, slimmer, lighter, etc."
"I can't find a good woman/man"
"men are dogs"
"women are just after what they can get"

You cannot be happy if you don't feel that you deserve happiness. It takes a conscious effort NOT to feel and speak unhappy statements like:
"why can't I be happy?"
"what's wrong with me?"

You must see yourself as you want to BE and from that point of being, you will attract what you desire. So the key is to consciously choose to feel good and then just stay in that feeling state. Remember the statement earlier that you attract people to you when your in a relationship? Because you are in a state of BEING in a loving relationship. And that it is difficult to find a mate when your single, it's because you are in a state of BEING single. Whatever state that you are in will attract more of it to you. Do not confuse being content in your state with being complacent, it takes conscious effort to move from where you are to where you want to be.

When you consciously choose to live in a state of thankfulness, you will automatically begin to feel good. It is not possible to think about the amazing things in your life and not feel good. By focusing on what is good, you will attract more good into your atmosphere. (In other words, if you act like a victim and focus on what is bad, more bad will come flooding your way). It sounds so simple... because it is.

I cannot stress enough the importance of focused thinking. Whether you focus your mind to simply calm yourself and feel a little more peace or if you do it to make conscious contact with your source, concentrating your thoughts in a specific area is an important tool when it comes to feeling good.

You can have it all. Anything your mind can conceive: money, health, love, and happiness. Which of these do you desire most? This will be your biggest problem. Which of these dreams do you want to manifest first? Because you can have them all using the law of attraction in the proper way. That is the key, knowing how to use this universal law properly to achieve any or all of your desires.

Improper use of the law of attraction will come back to harm you. Some women seem to believe that they would be a better mate for a particular man than his wife. They set their intensions on the man and constantly talk negative about his wife. Also, some men who desire to be successful in business desire for their competitor to be hindered in some way. Please think carefully before you purpose in your heart and mind to infringe on the life of another person.

Persistence is the key on how to manifest your desire; if

you are constantly working towards your goals and you have a burning desire to reach them you will eventually get to them. The only difference between someone who fails to reach their goals and someone who does not is that the one who succeeds keeps working towards their goals regardless of how many times they have failed. So have you ever failed in your life? Anyone who has attempted to accomplish anything in their lives can say that they have failed, yet they get back up and keep working towards what it is they desire.

There are simple and highly powerful meditation techniques that can automatically alter our vibrational state; breakdown resistance, obstacles, and old patterns of behavior. These easy and highly effective techniques put us in a vibrational match with the power of creation and create a quantum field of highly charged energy. It is by introducing our desire or intention into this quantum energy field that transforms us into a vibrational match with those desires and intentions that powerfully activates the law of attraction. Achieving a high energy vibrational match filled with intention and backed by powerful emotion is the secret to the art of successful manifesting.

If you are not currently manifesting what you desire, then there are two possibilities of why not: you are not clear and specific on what exactly it is you desire, or you are unaware of a certain belief that is contradicting your desire, and you must figure out what that belief is.

As you continue working towards your goals, do not be concerned as to how fast they manifest. The universe is constantly working to bring you what you desire; we as humans want everything to happen overnight. However, this is not how it works. Just keep your mind focused on what you want to experience; because the universe is constantly listening and will bring you whatever you ask for whether it is positive or negative.

Being Aware of What You Are Attracting

To bring what you desire into your physical reality, you have to be in vibrational harmony with it. And to be in vibrational harmony with your desire, you have to live your life as if you already have it and you are already enjoying it. The more you practice this, the faster you will be in the place of allowing your desire into your experience.

By paying attention to how you feel whenever you think of

your desire, you will be aware if your thoughts are in harmony with your desire. If you feel good whenever you think of what you desire, your thoughts and emotions are in line with what you want.

Your emotions play an important role because they can be a guide for you to know if your thoughts are a vibrational match to your desires.

You Get What You Think of - Whether You Like it Or Not.

Whatever you think about predominantly, you are going to get. Whether it is a good thing that dominates your thoughts or not, you will attract it. It is because the Law of Attraction is always at work. You must always be aware of what dominates your thoughts.

If you feel bad and worry most of the time, the universe will put people, circumstances, and events into your reality to give you the same feeling you have been putting out. That is why in manifesting your desires, feeling good is the key.

Always focus on your desire and feel good about it. The

more you think of what you want with a burning desire, the more swiftly it will manifest into your reality. Manifesting your desires with the help of the Law of Attraction can be done by aligning your thoughts with your emotions.

Remove any negative influences from your life. TV, for instance, is one of the worst sources for negative programming and could be considered as a hindrance to your ability to manifest. Also, try also to surround yourself with people who have a positive influence, avoid the negative people.

Tips for Manifesting Love Relationships Using the Law of Attraction

Look for any good traits in you. Note them down. Remind yourself often that you are a good and attractive person. Look into the mirror and find a loving and attractive person's image in it. Convince yourself that you are becoming a more attractive and confident person. Look for any negative traits and begin replacing them with good traits. Tell yourself constantly and believe that you are a worthy person and are capable of attracting the right person in your life who will love and respect you. As you are convinced by these powerful, loving thoughts, your subconscious mind, which believes and acts upon what you believe, begins the process of changing yourself!

The human mind, also known as the conscious mind, can influence the subconscious mind to change situations! The subconscious mind can be programmed to improve your image. You can easily change yourself into becoming an attractive person and can help you attract and hold love in your life. Like attracts like! This principle of the law of attraction works on the subconscious level. Properly programmed, this law can restructure your electromagnetic patterns and turn you into an irresistible person.

Do not use forceful thoughts while you are convincing yourself. The thought flow should be very smooth, and you should observe extreme calmness backed with complete faith in your conversation with your subconscious mind.

Feel that you're constantly sending out good and positive vibrations in all directions. Feel that these vibrations are filled with love and compassion for all. Visualize that these vibrations are engulfing every person that you meet.

Faithfully believe that the positive force that surrounds you makes you irresistible to others.

To attract love in your life, write down the **q**ualities that you are seeking. Believe that the person already exists, and destiny will bring you both together in due time, and you'll meet this lovely person very soon. You'll be amazed one day that you have attracted a person who possesses the exact qualities you desired! Your subconscious mind can attract the ideal person in your life if you let your subconscious mind know what you desire. Do not doubt the subconscious mind's ability to work wonders.

Three Tips for Using the Law of Attraction to Attract Your Desires

Holding an image in your mind is simple. It's determining what image you want to hold in your mind that is the hard part. An image that you hold in your mind is simply a picture of something that you haven't yet experienced. It's a vivid picture of something that you want or an experience that you'd like to have. Your mind doesn't know the difference between an imagined picture and a real experience. Therefore by holding an image in your mind, you begin sending thought vibrations into the universe.

Everything in the universe is vibrating, from the things that you are looking at right now to the thoughts in your head. When you hold an image in your mind, you begin the process of creating vibrations. The longer you hold those thoughts in your mind the better the quality of the thought vibrations. You've heard that the law of attraction works by sending thought vibrations into the universe, which returns those thought vibrations to you in the form of real physical goods. The best way to control what comes into your life is by the use of thought vibrations and mental imagery. Let's have a look at how expectation or belief and gratitude affect how you attract things into your life.

To manifest anything into your life, using the law of attraction, you have to expect that it will happen. The expectation is simply belief and belief is another word for faith. Faith believes in things not seen. When you combine expectation, belief, or faith with gratitude or Thanksgiving you have a powerful force. There is nothing stronger than belief. But when you combine belief with gratefulness and thankfulness, for whatever object that you hold in your mind, as though it has already happened or been received by you, then you are well on your way to having the desires of your heart.

CHAPTER 6

PRAYERS

I t is the VETERAN, not the preacher, who gave us the freedom of religion.

It is the VETERAN, not the reporter, who gave us the freedom of the press.

It is the VETERAN, not the poet, who gave us the freedom of speech.

It is the VETERAN, not the lawyer, who gave us the right to a fair trial.

It is the VETERAN, not the politician, who gave us the

right to vote.

It is the VETERAN, who salutes the flag and served under the flag, who gave us the freedom to proudly wave our flags.

***Courage to stand up to family/friends who take advantage**

Heavenly Father, I thank You for your gracious mercy towards me. I thank You that it is in You that I can find the courage and strength because Your Word says that God is our refuge and strength, a very present help in times of trouble. So Father, in times of family difficulties and challenges, I ask that You help me to find strength in You, to be able to stand to those family members and friends who take advantage of me in my time of sickness. I ask that You grant courage to enable me to forgive them their trespasses, as You will forgive me. Lord, when I feel that my family and friends are taking advantage of me, help me to look to You for guidance and protection because it is in You that I have everlasting peace. In Jesus Name, I pray, Amen.

Psalm 46:1, Matthew 6:14

***Not to fear being alone**

Father, I thank You that You have not given me a spirit of

fear, but of power and love and a sound mind. So, I shall not fear being alone, because I know that You are with me. Therefore, I trust in You because Your words are true and bring life. So, in the midst of loneliness, I am never alone. In times of weakness, You are my strength; whenever I fear, I am assured that You will uphold me with the right hand of Your righteousness. So, I thank You, Father, that when I feel afraid, I will trust in You because the Lord my God is with me wheresoever I may go. Therefore, I declare that because you are on my side, I will not fear what family or friends may do unto me. This is the prayer of my heart, in Jesus' Name, Amen.

2 Timothy 1:7, Isaiah 41:10, Psalm 56:3,

Joshua 1:9, Psalm 118:6

*Acknowledge their condition

Heavenly Father, You are omniscient, and there is nothing on this earth that You cannot fathom. I thank You because I can cast all my cares upon You because You care for me. So, in my permanent condition of an altered physical state, I know that you are my healer and there is nothing too hard for You. So right now, I believe Your report and know that you will make away for some assistance or assisted devices to make my life as great as possible where there is a physical deficiency. Your report says that by Your stripes I am healed; Your Word says that You will take away sickness from among us and You shall restore me to health in Jesus Name. So, I speak healing, because, in You, I shall be healed because You are the one I praise. Amen.

1 Peter 5:7, Isaiah 53:1, Isaiah 53:5, Jeremiah 17:14, Exodus 23:25, Jeremiah 30:17

***Not be Angry at Healthcare/Insurance Company for not providing coverage/denied coverage**

Dear Father, You are my shepherd, and I shall not want. So, I give You thanks and praise, in that during this time of sickness, I can turn to You because You are Jehovah Jireh, my provider. You know my wanderings through the wilderness, and because You have been with me, I have not lacked a thing. But God, as I am facing challenges with health care and Insurance companies not providing coverage and being denied access, help me to turn away from sinful anger and bitterness towards the healthcare policies and procedures because anger will not produce the righteousness that You desire. Help me to trust and rely on You, knowing my help comes from the Lord God Almighty, Creator of heaven and earth, Amen.

Psalm 23:1, Deuteronomy 2:7, James 1:20

***Go out in public and enjoy what's possible instead of hiding inside**

Heavenly Father, I give You thanks because Your Word reminds me that "the earth is the Lords and the fullness thereof. It is because of Your love towards humanity that I am free in You, because if the Son sets me free, I am free indeed. So Lord, despite my medical condition, help me not to feel bound by my current life circumstances. Help me not to remain closed in, hiding away from the beauty of Your creation; but Father, I ask that You help me to take pleasure in the public amenities and activities that You have created for me to enjoy. I walk in the freedom You have given me and not fear any unkind responses, but respond to them with intelligence and craftiness. In Jesus Name, Amen.

Psalm 24:1, John 8:36

***Move on from feeling betrayed by spouses/boyfriends who could not deal with their injury/illness and left them**

Dear loving Father, I am thankful because I am assured that You will never leave me or forsake me in times of difficulties, sickness or challenges because You have chosen me. Father, I know that You are always by my side; however, I feel betrayed by those who say they love and care for me but could not deal with the challenges of my condition. But Lord, help me to move on from those who have betrayed and hurt me during this time of injury/illness. You said, "Come to me, all who labor and are heavy laden, and I will give you rest." So, as I come to You, please heal my broken heart and bind up my wounds. In Jesus Name, Amen.

Deuteronomy 31:6, Psalm 147:3, Matthew 11:28

***Accept that in this lifetime they may not know "why" this happened**

Dear God, in this time of illness/injury and despair, I ask that You help me not to question Your power and authority continuously because You know all things. I may not know why I am going through this sickness/injury, but Father my trust and confidence is in You. One thing I am sure of is You have gone to prepare a place for me, and You will come again and receive me to Yourself, so where You are, there I may also be. So, Father, I may not know or understand why this has happened to me, but I will not let my heart be troubled because Your grace is sufficient for me, for Your power is made perfect in my weakness. Amen.

John 14:1-3, 2 Corinthians 12:9

CONCLUSION

This story shared the life of a soldier that experienced the greatest tragedy of his life after leaving a dangerous foreign war zone and returning to home ground.

We have seen that a doctor's professional opinion based on medical evidence is not always the accurate final outcome for patients.

When the Mind and Spirit form a divine collaboration then you are able overcome obstacles, setbacks and disappointments.

And that love set free that is meant to be will come back to you.

Often people make preparations for impending danger, but nobody on earth can predict nor avoid the events of fate that have been assigned to their life.

Every positive or negative situation that you experience is an important piece in the puzzle of life.

AUTHOR CONTACT

William and Tiffany, reside in the Chicagoland area, and they can be contacted through:

mindfulalert.com

www.linkedin.com/company/belle-mindful-resilience

REFERENCES

https://web.stanford.edu/class/e297c/war_peace/media/hpsych.html

https://abcnews.go.com/Health/MindMoodNews/story?id=7934145&page=1

https://www.inc.com/marla-tabaka/21-famous-quotes-to-honor-our-veterans-on-veterans-day.html

http://www.operationwearehere.com/VeteransFamiliesRecreation.html

https://www.blogs.va.gov/VAntage/1164/countering-negative-stereotypes-of-veterans/

https://www.bibletools.com

https://www.biblehub.com

https://www.biblegateway.com